First published in North America in 2021 by Boxer Books Limited.

www.boxerbooks.com

Boxer® is a registered trademark of Boxer Books Limited

Text and illustrations copyright © 2021 Sebastien Braun

The right of Sebastien Braun to be identified as the author

and illustrator of this work has been asserted by him

in accordance with the Copyright, Designs and Patents Act, 1988.

All rights reserved, including the right of reproduction in whole or in part in any form.

The illustrations were prepared in mixed media.

Library-of-Congress Cataloging-in-Publication Data available.

ISBN 978-1-912757-20-6

1 3 5 7 9 10 8 6 4 2

Printed in China

All of our papers are sourced from managed forests

and renewable resources.

To David,
for his trust
and support.
S.B.

I Love
My Home

Sebastien Braun

Boxer Books

I love my home in the forest.

It's my playground,
a place to have fun.

I love my home
in the treetops.

I can see
everything
from here.

I love my home underground where it is warm and snug.

I feel safe there with my family.

I love my
two homes.

One is in the cool river where I bathe and the other is on land where I graze.

I love my home
in the hay barn.

It's a great place
to play hide-and-seek!

I love my home in the ocean. It's my mysterious, underwater world.

I love my home in the precious coral beds.

Look at all
the colors.

I love my home
in the Savannah.

It is vast and I can roam where I like.

I love my home in the river.
We're adding branches
to make a dam.

I love my home in the air.
I love the freedom of
floating on the wind.

I love my home
in the trees.

Our nest is
in the branches.

I love my home
high in a hollow of a tree.
Day or night, it's the perfect
home for me.